Rapunzel's Tower
Three Bears' House
Three Little Pigs' Garden
Gingerbread Man's Bakery
Pied Piper's Music School & Exterminator, Inc.
Seven Dwarf Apartments
Goldilocks's Place
Fairy Supply Corp, Inc.

Once Upon a Slime

Written by Andy Maxwell
Illustrated by Samantha Cotterill

LB
Little, Brown and Company
New York Boston

Once upon a time,
Goldilocks visited her old friends, the Three Bears. Sure, they'd gotten off to a rocky start, what with the whole porridge thing. But by now, everyone was totally over it. "Plus," she thought, "who could stay mad at a girl with such beautiful golden locks?"

Goldilocks had just opened the bears' door when...

"EWW, GROSS!" Goldilocks yelled. "Okay, wise guys. Who did this?"

"Not me,"
Papa Bear said.

"I would never!"
Mama Bear said.

Goldilocks turned to Baby Bear.
"Then it had to be *you*! You're
still mad I broke your chair!"

"Baby Bear can't even reach that high!" Mama Bear said.

Goldilocks squinted suspiciously. "Hmph. Well, if it wasn't you, who did it?"

"I don't know." Papa Bear scratched his head. "Maybe Granny can help us? She loves a good mystery."

"Yay! It's a real whodunit!" said Baby Bear as they headed out to Granny's.

On the way, Goldilocks and the Three Bears ran into Little Red Riding Hood and the Big Bad Wolf having a picnic.

"Um, excuse me!" said Goldilocks. "Did you two see any creepy characters lurking around here? Somebody just *slimed* me at the bears' house!"

"Oh, hey, Goldie," Wolf mumbled. "Listen, Red and I are kinda busy here. Granny's *really* sick, and we gotta get this basket to her. Wish we could help and all, but—Oh! Granny! Uh, you're looking well!"

Granny was hustling up the path. “What’s that supposed to mean?” shouted Granny. “And get your paws off my cake!”

She lunged for her basket of goodies when...

"EWW, GROSS!"

wailed Little Red Riding Hood.

"Aw, why'd you ruin the cake, Granny?" whined Wolf. "I was eating that."

"You think I'd slime *myself*?" hollered Granny. "I didn't do this! I should potch you right in the schnozzle, Wolfie!"

"Take a chill pill, Granny," said Wolf.

As Granny wound up to sock him in the snout, Mama Bear broke up the scuffle.

"One sliming could be an accident," Papa Bear said. "But two? Someone is definitely up to *something*!"

Goldilocks had a brainstorm. "*Rapunzel*! She's always been out to get me!"

Before long, the gang arrived at Rapunzel's tower.

"Admit it, Rapunzel!" Goldie shouted. "It was *you* who slimed me! You've always been jealous of my beautiful curly locks."

Just as Goldilocks grabbed that long ponytail and gave it a good yank, Rapunzel herself strolled around the corner. "Hey, everyone!"

The group gasped.
"HUHHHH?"
If Rapunzel was standing right there, then whose hair was...

GUUUUUUUUUN
SPLOORP!

"EWW, GROSS!" everyone yelled.

"The sky is falling!" squeaked Baby Bear.

"Wrong fairy tale, Baby Bear," said Mama Bear.

"Hey, why'd ya slime us, Rapunzel?" Wolf demanded.

Rapunzel wiped a glob of gloop from her dress. "Me? *Ew!* I didn't! This stuff is disgusting!"

"But where did that fake hair come from?" Red wondered.

"It was a trap!" Goldilocks declared.

"Hey," said the wolf, "I know three little guys who know a lot about traps..."

And that's how they ended up at the Three Little Pigs' garden.

"Oh no! The wolf!" cried the littlest pig. "He'll huff and he'll puff—"

"Just cool your chinny chin chins, dudes," said Wolf. "Let's not forget which one of us got burned last time."

"Wait, you're *that* wolf too?" asked Red.

The wolf shrugged. "Hey, it's a living."

"Look," Goldilocks interrupted. "We're just trying to figure out who's been sliming everyone. Got any ideas?"

"How *dare* you!" the biggest pig snorted. "Just because we're pigs, when you hear the word 'slime,' you automatically think of us?"

Before Goldilocks could even respond...

SPSPSPSPSPLO
SPLIP. SPLIP. SSSPPPPPLLLO

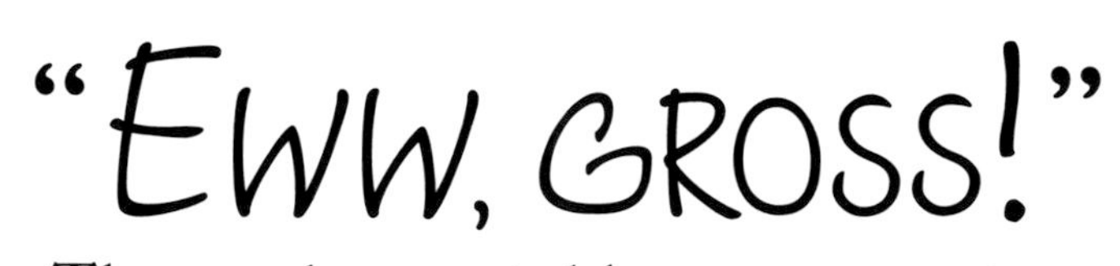

The garden sprinkler was spraying slime!

Everyone ran for cover.

"Aha! So it *was* you!" Wolf accused the pigs.

"It wasn't us! Somebody must have rigged it!" they protested.

Goldilocks shouted.

"No one's going *anywhere* until we figure this out.

"Let's break it down," Goldilocks began. "If it isn't any of the bears—although I'm still not a hundred percent sure about Baby Bear—and it's not Little Red Riding Hood or the Big Bad Wolf or Granny—"

"I sure wish I'd thought of it, though," said Granny.

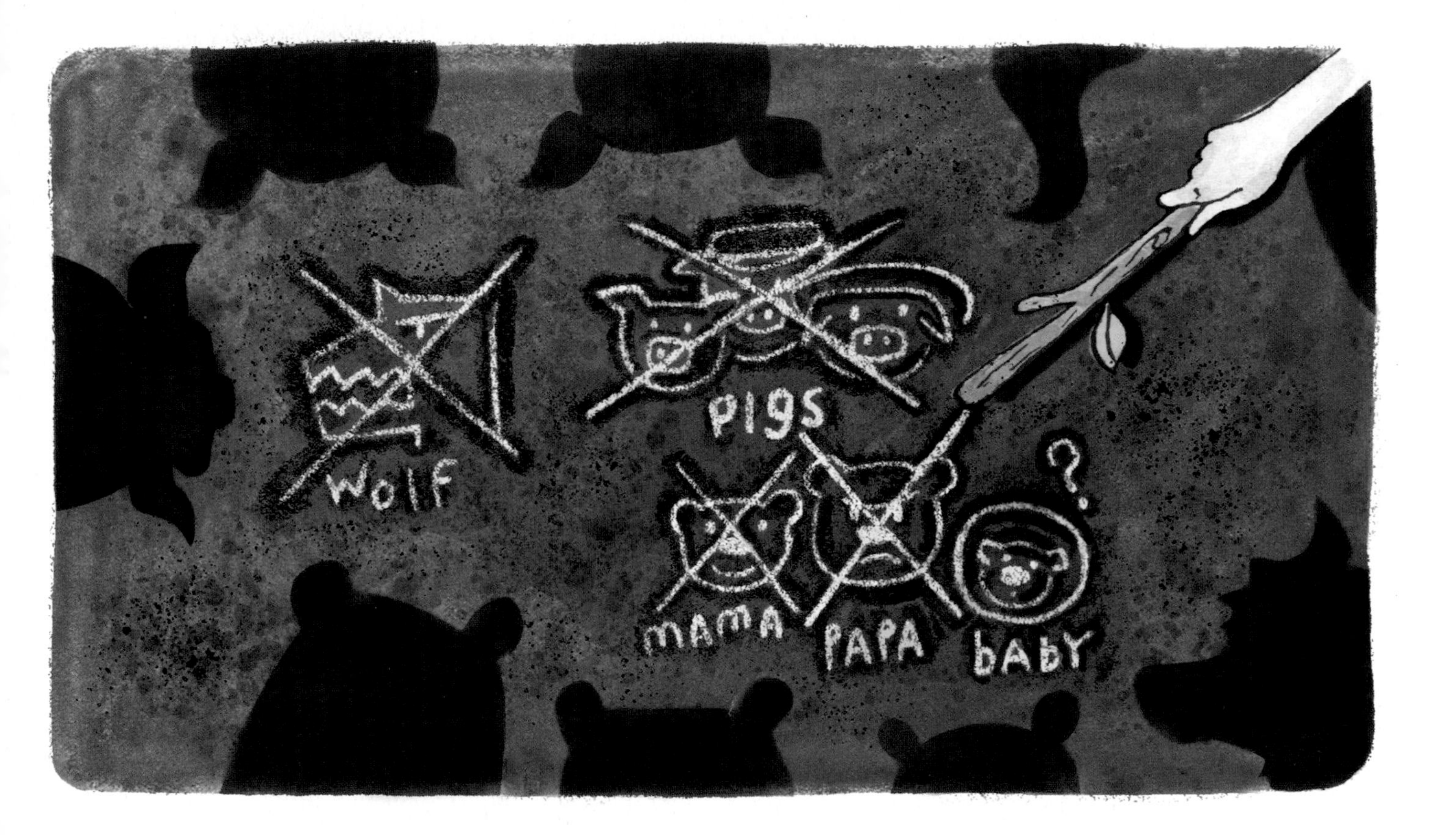

"And it's not Rapunzel, not the pigs...and it wasn't me..."

"Well, duh!" Rapunzel rolled her eyes.

"Who would think it's funny to see a bunch of fairy-tale folks getting slimed?" asked Goldilocks.

And that's when she realized there was one person they hadn't thought of.

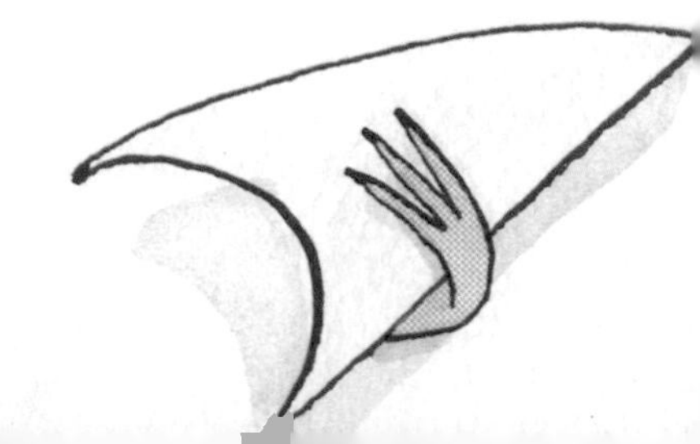

"IT WAS YOU! THE AUTHOR!" Goldilocks accused. "You slimed us!"

"Me?" said the author. "What? No. That's crazy!"

"He made me live in a straw house!" whined one of the pigs.

"And he made a prince climb up my hair like a rope!" said Rapunzel.

"And he made you lousy kids eat all my cake," Granny said. "I oughta potch *him* in the schnozzle!"

"Guys, guys!" the author broke in. "Look. Yes, *fine*, I *did* write the story. So I guess in that way, *technically*, I did *kind of* slime you. But I couldn't *actually* slime you. I mean, I'm not even *in* the story, right?"

"Ugh! *Whatever*. I get it," Goldilocks said. "But then who *did* do it? Because we're totally out of suspects!"

Suddenly, there was a mighty croak. "Oh, NO, you're not!"

At their feet stood a small frog wearing a crown. "Who *did* it, you ask? 'Twas I, the Frog Prince! I confess! At last, I have seen my revenge upon all of you!"

The frog cleared his throat. "Let's start with you, 'Big Bad Wolf'! Pretending to be king of the forest when I, the Frog Prince, am the true heir to the throne!

"And you, Rapunzel! Remember that day I tried to croak a duet with you and you pushed me off the tower? That really hurt!

"As for Grandmother, I'm terribly sorry. I was actually going for Baby Bear, who had nearly stepped on me last spring. But *you*, Little Pigs, you poke fun at my slimy pond—when you literally, *literally* live in a pigsty!

"Then there's *you*, Goldilocks." The frog wiped away a gloopy tear. "Oh, Goldilocks, you hurt me the most!

"You could have been my princess," the frog said wistfully.
"All I desired was a kiss to free me of this curse, but, alas...!

"And so I have taken *great pleasure* in drenching each of you with slime from my pond to teach you an important lesson about honesty, dignity, and honor!"

Everyone was speechless.

"Wow," said Red finally. "Anybody here know how to speak Frog? It really seems like this fella is trying to tell us something, doesn't it?"

Goldilocks bent down and picked up the frog. "It's okay, little guy. Come here. Let me give you a smooch."

"I don't want your kiss!" croaked the Frog Prince, as Goldilocks puckered up. "I want revenge!"

With her kiss, the Frog Prince turned back into a regular prince.

"*Ahem*. As I was saying..." the prince continued. "'Twas I, the Frog Prince, who slimed you."

There was an awkward moment.

"Wait a minute. You're a *prince*?" said Goldilocks, eyeing him. "Like, with a whole kingdom to rule? You know, I'd be *really* great at that!" She kissed him again.

"Eww, *gross*," said Rapunzel.

"That's...messed up," Wolf said.

"I guess all's well that ends well," said Papa Bear.

"Is there any more cake?" Granny asked nobody in particular.

And so they all lived happily ever after....

Or, in the case of Goldilocks and her prince, *slimily* ever after.

THE END

For Sabine and Nate, who brought so much ~~slime~~ love into our lives —AM

For Mum and Dad, even though you made me clean my room —SC

ABOUT THIS BOOK The illustrations for this book were done in ink on watercolor paper and then digitally colored. This book was edited by Andrea Spooner and designed by Saho Fujii and Nicole Brown. The production was supervised by Erika Schwartz, and the production editor was Jen Graham. The text was set in Windsor, the display type is Mesa, and the slime type was hand-lettered by Ricardo Velazquez.

 Little, Brown and Company • Hachette Book Group • 1290 Avenue of the Americas, New York, NY 10104 • Visit us at LBYR.com • First Edition: July 2018 • Little, Brown and Company is a division of Hachette Book Group, Inc. • The Little, Brown name and logo are trademarks of Hachette Book Group, Inc. • The publisher is not responsible for websites (or their content) that are not owned by the publisher. • Library of Congress Cataloging-in-Publication Data • Names: Maxwell, Andy, author. | Cotterill, Samantha, illustrator. • Title: Once upon a slime / written by Andy Maxwell ; illustrated by Samantha Cotterill. • Description: First edition. | New York ; Boston : Little, Brown and Company, 2018. | Summary: Beginning with Goldilocks, various fairy-tale characters are drenched in slime and join forces to discover who is responsible. • Identifiers: LCCN 2016038900 | ISBN 9780316393263 (hardcover) | ISBN 9780316393270 (ebook) • Subjects: | CYAC: Characters in literature—Fiction. | Humorous stories. • Classification: LCC PZ7.1.M3844 Onc 2018 | DDC [E]—dc23 • LC record available at https://lccn.loc.gov/2016038900 • ISBNs: 978-0-316-39326-3 (hardcover), 978-0-316-51040-0 (ebook), 978-0-316-51042-4 (ebook), 978-0-316-51041-7 (ebook) • 10 9 8 7 6 5 4 3 2 1 • APS • PRINTED IN CHINA

Prince Charming & Snow White-Charming's Castle
Jack's Artisanal Beanstalkery
Grandma Riding Hood's House
Big Bad Wolf's Trailer
Frog Prince Pond
Definitely not Wicked Witch's House
Old Woman's Boot and